Timothy Goes to School

Dial Books for Young Readers

NEW YORK

TIMOTHY GOES TO SCHOOL

Story and pictures by

Rosemary Wells

For Jennifer and Karen H.

Published by
Dial Books for Young Readers
A division of Penguin USA Inc.
375 Hudson Street, New York, New York 10014

Copyright © 1981 by Rosemary Wells
All rights reserved
Printed in Hong Kong by South China Printing Company (1988) Limited
Designed by Jane Byers Bierhorst
E / 10 9 8 7

Library of Congress Cataloging in Publication Data
Wells, Rosemary / Timothy goes to school.
Summary: Timothy learns about being accepted and making
friends during the first week of his first year at school.
[1. School stories.] I. Title.
PZ7.W46843Ti   [E]   80-20785
ISBN 0-8037-8948-3 / ISBN 0-8037-8949-1 (lib. bdg.)

*The full-color artwork consists of black line-drawings
and full-color washes. The black line is prepared
and photographed separately for greater sharpness and
contrast. The full-color washes are prepared with
watercolors. They are then camera-separated and
reproduced as red, yellow, blue, and black halftones.*

Timothy's mother made him a brand-new sunsuit for the first day
of school.

"Hooray!" said Timothy.

Timothy went to school in his new sunsuit with his new book and his new pencil.

"Good morning!" said Timothy.

"Good morning!" said the teacher.

"Timothy," said the teacher, "this is Claude.

Claude, this is Timothy. I'm sure you'll be the best of friends."

"Hello!" said Timothy.

"Nobody wears a sunsuit on the first day of school," said Claude.

During playtime Timothy hoped and hoped that
Claude would fall into a puddle.

But he didn't.

When Timothy came home, his mother asked, "How was
school today?"

"Nobody wears a sunsuit on the first day of school," said Timothy.

"I will make you a beautiful new jacket," said Timothy's mother.

Timothy wore his new jacket the next day.

"Hello!" said Timothy to Claude.

"You're not supposed to wear party clothes
on the second day of school," said Claude.

All day Timothy wanted and wanted Claude to make a mistake.

But he didn't.

When Timothy went home, his mother asked, "How did it go?"

"You're not supposed to wear party clothes on the second day of school," said Timothy.

"Don't worry," said Timothy's mother. "Tomorrow you just wear something in-between like everyone else."

The next day Timothy went to school in his favorite shirt.

"Look!" said Timothy. "You are wearing the same shirt I am!"

"No," said Claude, "you are wearing the same shirt that *I* am."

During lunch Timothy wished and wished that Claude
would have to eat all alone.

But he didn't.

After school Timothy's mother could not find Timothy. "Where are you?" she called.

"I'm never going back to school," said Timothy.

"Why not?" called his mother.

"Because Claude is the smartest and the best at everything and he
has all the friends," said Timothy.

"You'll feel better in your new football shirt," said Timothy's
mother.

Timothy did not feel better in his new football shirt.

That morning Claude played the saxophone.

"I can't stand it anymore," said a voice next to Timothy.

It was Violet.

"You can't stand what?" Timothy asked Violet.

"Grace!" said Violet. "She sings. She dances. She counts up to a thousand and she sits next to me!"

During playtime Timothy and Violet stayed together.

Violet said, "I can't believe you've been here all along!"
"Will you come home and have cookies with me after school?"
Timothy asked.

On the way home Timothy and Violet laughed so much about
Claude and Grace that they both got the hiccups.